When I am Quiet on O'ahu

by Judi Riley

Hawai'i is home to some of the most rare and endangered animals in the world.

Open your senses and drift into a world of make-believe encounters with some unusual animal friends.

But remember to tell your keiki (kay-key, child) that in real life, it is important to admire wildlife from afar.

For: Kundera and Tiki... keep a cloud warm for us, we miss you immensely

Look for more Tiki Tales:

When I am Quiet on Maui

When I am Quiet on Kaua'i

When I am Quiet on the Big Island

A not-so-Quiet Thanks for Inspiration, Guidance and Ballast to: Charlie, The Rileys, The Meolas, Pat and The Quintessas, The Morrisons, The Wagners, The Kona Mamas, Kentaro, Steven, Ken, The Zieglers, and the Boo Boo Zoo, Dick, Doug, Vicki, The Benjamins, Larry, Kevin, The Simmons, The Nelsons, Pazya, Robyn, Joanie, Aunt Glenda, Margaret,

©2005

Published by Judi Riley's Tiki Tales

P.O. Box 1194, Haiku, Hi 96708

www.TikiTales.com

ISBN 0-9740582-2-X

Printed and Bound in China

When you are quiet,

what do you hear?

When you are still,

what do you see?

When I am quiet
in Waikīkī as the day breaks,
I hear the legendary Duke Kahanamoku
welcome the morning waves.

Waikīkī *(Why-key-key)*
Duke Kahanamoku *(Kah-haw-nah-mow-koo)* – Hawaiian surfer and Olympic gold
medalist, a statue of him fronts Waikīkī Beach

When I stand still by the Stones of Life,
a pīkake pauses next to me
with his stunning blues and greens,
and shakes his tail feathers,
like an expert hula dancer.

pīkake *(pee-kah-keh)* — peacock, Princess Kaʻiulani's favorite pet

· HONOLULU ZOO ·

The best zoo for 2300 miles in any direction

Calgary Zoo   2745 mi

Ueno Zoo   3950 mi

Seattle Zoo   2678 mi

Seoul Zoo 3980 mi

Toronto Zoo   far

Peking Zoo   4850 mi

Los Angeles Zoo 2567 mi

New Delhi Zoo 7300 mi

San Diego Zoo 2511

When I am quiet
at the Honolulu Zoo an hour after eight,
I hear an Asian elephant call
to a Sumatran tiger.

Honolulu *(Hoh-no-loo-loo)*
Asian elephant – endangered
Sumatran tiger – critically endangered

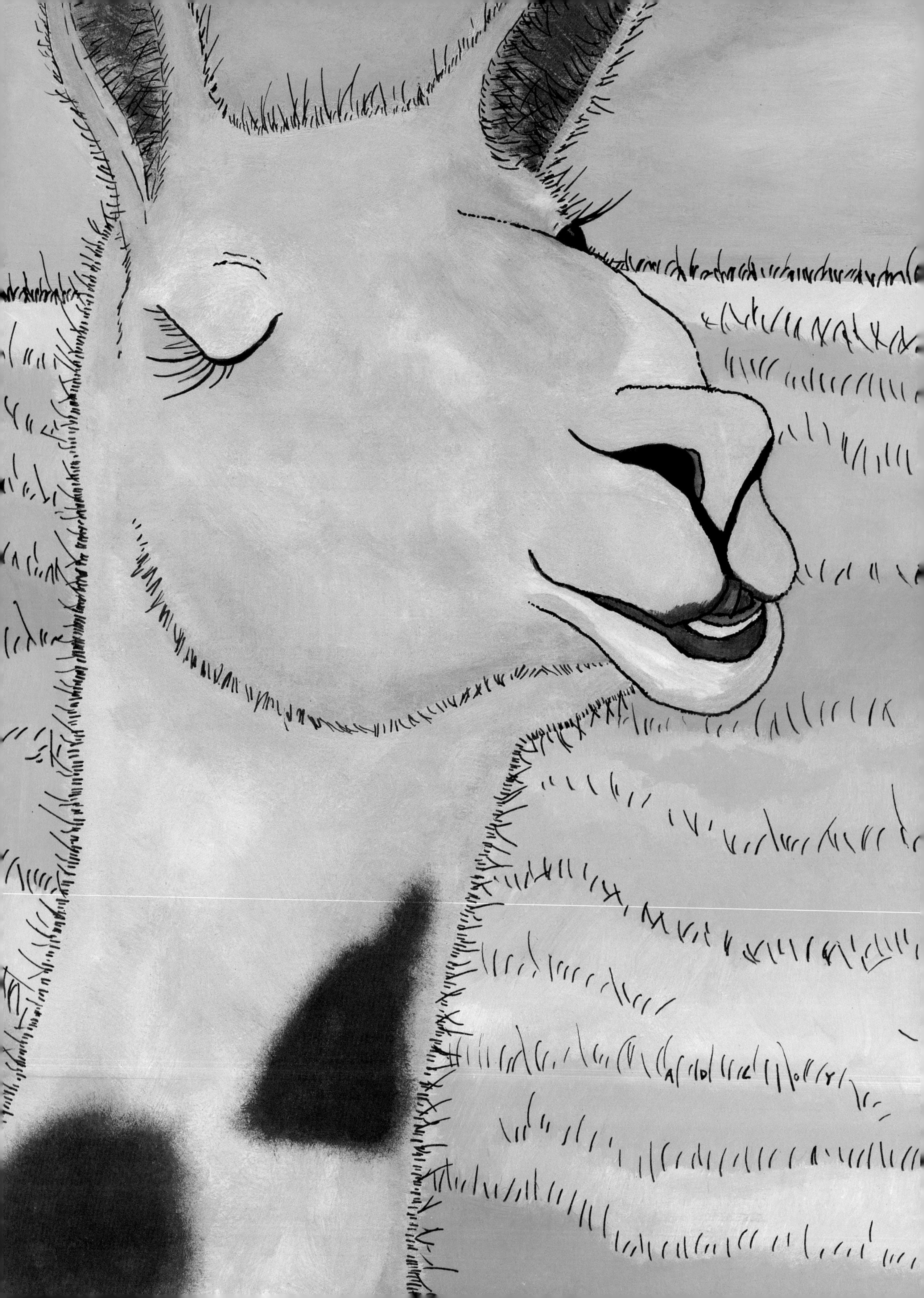

When I stand still by a llama,
she reassures me
with a nod to the past,
and a wink to tomorrow,
like warm sunshine after the rain.

When I am quiet
in Kāneʻohe a bit before brunch,
I hear the boats
bob in the bay.

Kāneʻohe *(Kah-nay-oh-hay)*

When I stand still in the grass,

a pueo swoops past my sunhat,

with his soundless wings

and effortlessly sails into the sunlight,

like an outrigger canoe on calm seas.

pueo *(poo-ay-oh)* – the sacred Hawaiian short eared owl is diurnal (active during the day)
outrigger – Hawaiian canoe
hulu *(who-loo)* – feather

will the shadow come at 12:01?

When I am quiet
at Queen Emma's Summer Palace
right around noon,
I hear a shadow sigh
before taking a stretch.

Queen Emma – wife of King Kamehameha IV

When I sit still on Queen Emma's lānai,

a puppy cuddles me

with her cottony curls

then snuggles up to my toes,

like a plush loke lani blossom.

lānai *(lah-nye)* – porch
loke lani *(low-keh law-nee)* – pink rose

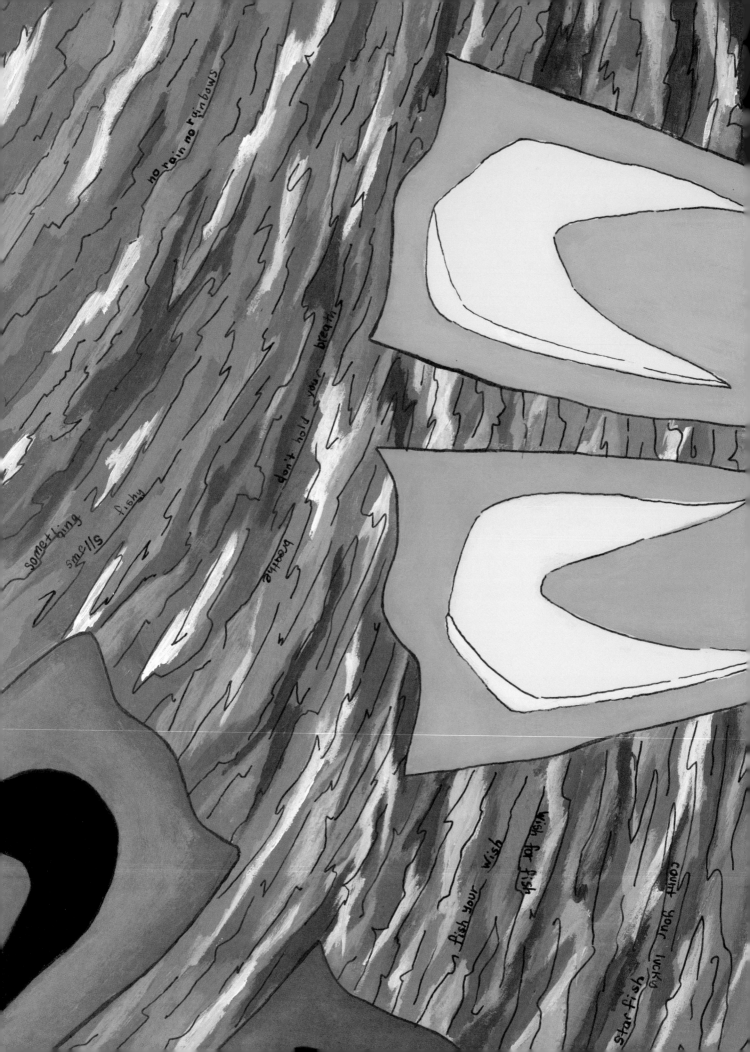

When I am quiet
at Hanauma Bay two days after Tuesday,
I hear a rainbow of snorkelers
explore the reef.

Hanauma *(Hah-now-mah)*

When I float still above the limu,
the lauwiliwili smile below me
in a lemony swirl,
and linger near my flippers,
like butterflies in a breeze.

limu *(lee-moo)* – seaweed
Lauwiliwili *(l-ow-wee-lee-wee-lee)* – Lemon Butterfly Fish, found only in Hawai'i

When I am quiet
in Waimea Valley at four-forty-four,
I hear the flit-flit-flutter
of the paper bark trees.

Waimea *(Why-may-ah)*
paper bark trees – its bark peels, then dangles in paper-thin layers

When I am stand still in the sanctuary,
the moorhens mesmerize me
with their "erk, erk, orks",
and the ease with which they swim,
like mermaids of the marsh.

Hawaiian moorhen – endangered and native to Hawai'i

When I am quiet
on the north shore
as the sun slips into the sea,
I hear the surf reach for the sky.

When I lie still on the beach,
a sleepy monk seal moves next to me,
and nestles in the sand,
like driftwood waiting for the tide.

Hawaiian monk seal – endangered, found only in Hawai'i

When I am quiet
in my room at twilight,
I hear an Oʻahu Oʻo
in the ʻōhiʻa tree,
singing to the stars.

Oʻahu Oʻo *(Oh-ah-who Oh-oh)* – Yellow-tufted Honeyeater, sadly extinct
ʻōhiʻa lehua tree *(oh-hee-ah lay-who-ah)* – sacred native Hawaiian tree

When I lie still on my bed,

a coot and a stilt fluff up the pillows

with their gorgeous black wings,

then we duck into dreamtime,

like bare feet in warm sand.

Hawaiian stilt or Ae'o *(Eye-oh)* – Endangered
Hawaiian coot or 'Alae ke'oke'o *(Ah-lye kay-oh-kay-oh)* – Endangered

When you are quiet,
what do you hear?

When you are still,
don't forget to look all around you.

A hui hou kākou.

a hui hou kākou (*ah who-ee-ho kah-koh*) – until we meet again

Glossary

(in order of appearance)

Duke Kahanamoku *(Kah-haw-nah-mow-koo)* – legendary Hawaiian surfer and Olympic gold medalist

pīkake *(pee-kah-keh)* – peacock, Princess Ka'iulani's favorite pet

pueo *(poo-ay-oh)* – sacred Hawaiian short eared owl

outrigger – Hawaiian canoe

hulu *(who-loo)* – feather

Queen Emma – wife of King Kamehameha IV

lānai *(lah-nye)* – porch

loke lani *(low-keh law-nee)* – pink rose

limu *(lee-moo)* – seaweed

lauwiliwili *(l-ow-wee-lee-wee-lee)* – Lemon Butterfly Fish, found only in Hawai'i

Hawaiian monk seal – endangered, fewer than 1,500 exist – if you are lucky enough to see one resting on the beach, please keep your distance

O'ahu O'o *(Oh-ah-who Oh-oh)* – Yellow-tufted Honeyeater, sadly extinct

'ōhi'a lehua tree *(oh-hee-ah lay-who-ah)* – sacred native Hawaiian tree

Hawaiian stilt or Ae'o *(Eye-oh)* – endangered

Hawaiian coot or 'Alae ke'oke'o *(Ah-lye kah-oh-kah-oh)* – endangered

a hui hou kākou *(ah who-ee-ho kah-koh)* – until we meet again